Jimmy Gownley's

AMELiA RULES!™

THE WHOLE WORLD'S CRAZY

Atheneum Books for Young Readers
New York   London   Toronto   Sydney

· Special thanks to Michael Cohen ·

Atheneum Books for Young Readers
An imprint of Simon & Schuster Children's Publishing Division
1230 Avenue of the Americas, New York, New York 10020
Book design by Jimmy Gownley and Sonia Chaghatzbanian
First Atheneum Books for Young Readers paperback edition May 2009
Manufactured in China
1014 SCP
8 10 9 7
CIP data for this is book is available from the Library of Congress.
ISBN: 978-1-4169-8604-1

These comics were originally published individually by Renaissance Press.

With Love and Thanks
to Mom and Dad...

With appreciation for
the Vision and Faith of
Joe, John, Jerry, and Bill...

And with gratitude for
the Patience and Friendship
of Michael...

This book is dedicated with love...
for Karen.

Amelia vs.
the Sneeze Barf

Jimmy Gownley's

AMELIA RULES!™

HEY, HOW'S IT GOING? BEAUTIFUL NIGHT, ISN'T IT?

SORRY MY ROOM IS SUCH A MESS!

WE JUST MOVED, SO I HAVEN'T GOT AROUND TO FIXING THINGS UP YET.

ACTUALLY, WE'VE BEEN HERE FOR TWO MONTHS AND MOM'S BEEN HAVING A FIT FOR ME TO CLEAN UP!

OH, I DON'T MEAN TO BE RUDE...

C'MON IN!

THINGS ARE OKAY HERE. I MET THIS ONE BOY...REGGIE... WHO I LIKE...WELL NOT LIKE *THAT!* BOYS ARE GROSS!

OH, AN' THERE'S THIS *GIRL RHONDA?* SHE HATES ME! I THINK IT'S CUZ SHE LIKES REGGIE...I MEAN, *LIKES HIM* LIKES HIM.

I GUESS YOU SHOULD KNOW MY PARENTS SPLIT...UP.

THAT'S HOW COME ME AN' MOM MOVED IN HERE WITH AUNT TANNER.

THE WHOLE THING IS KINDA WEIRD AN' IT MADE ME FEEL... I DON'T KNOW...GUILTY? SO I ASKED MOM IF I WAS THE REASON THEY GOT DIVORCED. SHE GOT REAL NERVOUS AN' TRIED TO MAKE A JOKE. SHE SAID...

"IF *THAT WERE* TRUE, WE WOULD'VE BROKEN UP YEARS AGO."

THAT'S ONE THING I'VE NOTICED ABOUT GROWN-UPS...

THEY'RE NOT FUNNY.

5

SO... UMM... THANKS FOR LETTIN' US WATCH YOUR TV!

SURE.

SO WHAT ARE WE WATCHING AGAIN?

INTERGALACTIC NINJA FIGHT SQUADRON!

WE'D WATCH AT MY HOUSE, BUT WE DON'T HAVE CABLE... AN' PAJAMAMAN DOESN'T EVEN HAVE A TV!

YOU'RE KIDDING.

NOPE! IT'S LIKE AN *AMISH* FUNERAL PARLOR.

WOW.

KNOCK KNOCK KNOCK

WHO IN THE WORLD COULD THAT BE?

RHONDA?! WHAT ARE *YOU* DOING HERE?

REGGIE INFORMED ME THAT I'D BEEN INVITED... BUT I GUESS I'LL JUST TURN *AROUND.*

OKAY, WELL... WE'LL SEE YA! SO LONG! DON'T FORGET TO WRITE!

HEY!

8

9

i'm doomed...

IF I PAY *RHONDA* A NICKEL A DAY, I'LL BE *BROKE!* I WON'T BE ABLE TO BUY *CANDY* OR *COMIC BOOKS* OR SAVE FOR *COLLEGE!*

WELL, IF IT MAKES YOU FEEL ANY BETTER, YOU PROBABLY WEREN'T GOING TO *COLLEGE* ANYWAY.

BUT I'LL TELL YOU *WHAT*... WHY DON'T *I* PAY RHONDA EVERY DAY *FOR* YOU.

REALLY?!

SURE! AN' ALL *YOU* HAVE TO DO IS GIVE ME FIFTY CENTS EVERY *SATURDAY!*

HMM...

THAT WAY, YOU ONLY PAY ONCE A WEEK, WHICH IS *SIX TIMES LESS!*

WOW!

SEE, BUDDY, WHO TAKES CARE OF YA?

GEE, *AMELIA,* I DON'T KNOW *WHAT I'D DO! WITHOUT YOU!*

HEY! WHAT ARE *PALS* FOR?

20

21

AH AH **AHH CHOOOOOOOOO**

MEANWHILE... IN THE BACKYARD OF MILD-MANNERED *REGGIE GRABINSKY.*

ALL RIGHT, TEAM! WELCOME TO G.A.S.P.* HEADQUARTERS.

G.A.S.P.

* GATHERING OF AWESOME SUPER PALS

YES, *G.A.S.P.!* THE EXTRAORDINARY CRIME-FIGHTING TEAM LED BY THE MIGHTY... *CAPTAIN AMAZING!*

WITH HIS *PARTNERS:* *KID LIGHTNING,* WHOSE AMAZING SPEED MAKES HIM A *WHIRLING DERVISH* OF PAIN.

PRINCESS POWERFUL, THE DAZZLING BEAUTY WHO ENCHANTS THE BOYS, EVEN AS SHE BASHES THEM.

AND FINALLY... THE MYSTERIOUS LONER KNOW ONLY AS... THE MOUTH

THE NAME IS MS. MIRACULOUS.

LET'S GET THIS SHOW ON THE ROAD!

23

AHCHOOOoo

YOU POOR THING! ARE YOU OKAY?

IT'S MY ALLERGIES... I'M FEELING BETTER TODAY, BUT LAST NIGHT I ALMOST SNEEZE BARFED!

OH, PLEASE PLEASE *PLEASE* DON'T LET HER ASK...

WHAT THE HECK IS A "SNEEZE BARF"?!

WHAT'S A SNEEZE BARF?

OH, WELL...

WELL, IT'S KINDA HARD TO EXPLAIN... BUT LET'S SEE...

Sneezicus Barfona (the Common Sneeze Barf) can occur to anyone at any time (fig. 1). Early symptoms include sniffles and a strong feeling of dread (fig. 2). Gradually one becomes aware of a strange queasiness combined with the urge to never again eat at Taco Bell (fig. 3).

COULD BE YOU

(fig.1)

sniff sniff

Uh-oh

(fig.2)

TACO BELL

(fig.3)

Soon the queasiness grows more intense and the nostrils begin to burn (fig. 4).

Often at this point the victim bravely tries to stifle the twin urges (fig. 5).

This soon proves futile and so... (fig. 6).

SNIFF GNNF GNNF GNNF

AHH BLAH THEEEW

(fig.4)   (fig.5)   (fig.6)

IT'S A CONDITION THAT HAS BROUGHT MODERN MEDICINE TO ITS *KNEES!*

HMM...

CAN WE GET THIS SHOW ON THE ROAD... I GOT *HOMEWORK!*

OKAY, OKAY, OKAY...

KID LIGHTNING, LIGHTS, PLEASE.

NOW, PLEASE PAY CLOSE ATTENTION TO THE FOLLOWING TOP-SECRET SLIDE PRESENTATION.

I HAD NO IDEA THIS CLUBHOUSE WAS *MULTIMEDIA!*

CLICK

OUR SUBJECTS GO BY THE NAMES BUG AND IGGY.

I HAVE CLASS WITH THE SHORT ONE.... HE SMELLS.

THEY'VE BEEN MENACING KIDS FOR YEARS.

CLICK

AND NOW WE MUST *LOOK!*

NYAHAHAHAHAHA

♪ REGGIE GOT A WEDGIE ♪ REGGIE GOT A WEDGIE

YOU **GOOBER!** YOU **ARE** REGGIE!

YEAH, *DOOFUS!* WHAT THE HECK IS WRONG WITH YOU?

WHY WON'T THEY JUST GIVE YOU A WEDGIE AN' ROB YOU AGAIN?

I'M WEARING A CAPE.

UNCONVINCED, THE MIGHTY MEMBERS OF G.A.S.P. START OUT ON THEIR DREADFUL *MISSION....*

UNTIL SUDDENLY...

♪ **REGGIE!** I HAVE SNACKS ♫ FOR YOU AND YOUR FRIENDS!

PTWING!

27

AND SO... THIRTY MINUTES, TWELVE RING DINGS, THIRTY-SIX COOKIES, EIGHT HO-HOS AND, FOUR EGG CREAMS LATER...

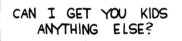

CAN I GET YOU KIDS ANYTHING ELSE?

no, please, have mercy...

WELL, THANKS, REGGIE. I'LL CATCH YOU GUYS LATER.

WHAT!

BUT WHAT ABOUT OUR MISSION? WHAT ABOUT MY REVENGE?

I MEAN, JUSTICE!

I TOLD YOU I GOT HOMEWORK!

OH PLEASE, AMELIA! PLEASE PLEASE PLEASE!

OKAY! FINE!

YES!

BUT IF AMELIA FLUNKS SOCIAL STUDIES...

PRINCESS POWERFUL IS GONNA KICK YOUR BUTT!

NO ONE'S CERTAIN WHAT HAPPENED NEXT. PERHAPS IT WAS THE GLARING LATE AFTERNOON SUN. PERHAPS IT WAS THE ALLERGIES. IT ALMOST CERTAINLY WAS THE SNACK FOOD. REGARDLESS, THE NEXT INSTANT WOULD BE BURNED INTO THESE FIVE YOUNG MINDS ... FOREVER.

BY THE TIME REGGIE GOT DONE YAKKING EVERYWHERE, IT WAS GETTING PRETTY LATE. I REALLY HAD TO BOOK TO GET HOME ON TIME, BUT I DIDN'T MIND RUNNING CUZ I WAS SO EXCITED.

I KNEW REGGIE WOULD DIE IF TANNER FOUND OUT WHAT HAPPENED, SO I COULDN'T WAIT TO TELL HER.

BUT WHEN I GOT HOME, EVERYTHING CHANGED.

OH, DON'T GIVE ME THAT! YOU LIAR!

I KNEW MOM WAS TALKING TO DAD. SHE DIDN'T TALK THAT WAY TO ANYONE ELSE. I HATED TO HEAR THEM LIKE THIS, AND NOW THAT WE'VE MOVED, IT'S EVEN WORSE, CUZ THEY DON'T HAVE TO FACE EACH OTHER.

AMELIA!

!

OH... TANNER!

UMM...C'MON, SHRIMP. LET'S GET OUTTA HERE! HEY! HOW ABOUT I PLAY YOU MY NEW SONG?

OH...UMM... OKAY.

I HOPE YOU'RE HAPPY!

amelia HEARD us, THAT'S what i'm TALKING about!

WE WENT UP TO TANNER'S ROOM AN' SHE STARTED PLAYING FOR ME, BUT I WASN'T LISTENING. I COULDN'T STOP THINKING ABOUT WHAT I HEARD...WHAT WAS GOING ON.

>SIGH<

"I USED TO BE DISGUSTED, NOW I TRY TO BE AMUSED."

WHAT?

ELVIS COSTELLO... FIRST ALBUM.

BUT TANNER DIDN'T LET ME MOPE FOR LONG.

YOU KNOW, AMELIA, JUST BECAUSE YOUR HOME IS BROKEN...

THAT DOESN'T MEAN YOU HAVE TO BE.

UMM... TH-THANKS.

THANKS, TANNER.

DON'T MENTION IT. NOW DO YOU WANNA HEAR THIS SONG?

SURE.

YOU'LL LIKE IT. IT'S GOT LYRICS YOU'RE TOO YOUNG TO HEAR.

TANNER PLAYED A BUNCH OF SONGS FOR ME, AND IT WAS NICE. SHE PLAYS REALLY PRETTY.

AND I THOUGHT A LOT ABOUT WHAT SHE SAID, AND I GUESS IT'S TRUE. IT'S JUST HARD TO REMEMBER SOMETIMES.

PLUS, I DON'T WANT TO HAVE TO REMEMBER! I JUST WANT THE WHOLE STUPID THING FIXED, OR AT LEAST OVER! BUT I KNOW THAT'S STUPID, AND I'M JUST BEING A BABY, SO I'LL BE TOUGH.....AND I *CAN* BE! YOU *WATCH!* I JUST... »YAWN«...I JUST WISH IT DIDN'T MAKE ME SO...SO...TIRED

ZZZZZ

The Gym
Class System

HEY! WHAT'S UP?

I'M GLAD YOU STOPPED BY. I NEEDED A *BREAK!*

I'VE BEEN STUDYING FOR THIS SOCIAL STUDIES TEST. IT'S THE *THIRD* ONE IN *TWO WEEKS*...I THINK THE WOMAN IS CRACKED!

TO TELL YOU THE *TRUTH*...

THE WHOLE *SCHOOL* IS A LITTLE *OFF*...

I NOTICED IT THE FIRST DAY.

I HATE SCHOOL! WHY CANT WE HAVE THE APOCALYPSE INSTEAD.

KEEP YAKKIN' AND YOU'LL *GET* IT!

39

SO, WHY ARE WE JUST **STANDING** HERE? **INTRODUCE** ME!

WHY **BOTHER?** THEY'RE ALL JUST A BUNCHA **JERKS!**

LIKE, YOU SEE THAT CREW OVER **THERE?**

THEY'RE THE **BRAINY** KIDS...YOU KNOW... STRAIGHT A'S... ALWAYS BLOWING THE **CURVE.**

TOTALLY STUCK UP!

OOOKAY...WELL, WHAT ABOUT **THOSE** GUYS?

ARE YOU **KIDDING** ME?! THE **JOCKS?!** **FORGET** IT!

THE WAY THEY'RE ALL **COORDINATED** AN' EVERYTHING! I KNOW THEY DO IT TO **SPITE** ME!

REGGIE, BUDDY, YA GOT **ISSUES.**

OKAY, LET'S **SEE...**

WHAT ABOUT **THEM?** BROWN NOSERS!

THEM? TEACHERS' PETS!

THEM? YIKES! BAND MEMBERS!

THEM? FASHION PLATES!

>HEH HEH< LOOKS LIKE THEY'RE ALL HERE, ALL RIGHT!

YEP... ALL THE **STANDARD** GROUPS!

EXCEPT YOU DIDN'T MENTION THE **NERDS!** >HEH HEH<

DO YOU GUYS HAVE ANY... umm ANY **NERDS?**

oh no.

42

43

44

WHO SAID...!

HMMPH!!

RING RING RING RING

COME IN! COME IN, EVERYONE....

PLEASE, EVERYONE FIND A **SEAT!**

C'MON, THERE'S STILL SEATS IN THE BACK.

>AHEM< WELCOME! WELCOME, YOUNG STUDENTS, TO THE ADVENTURE WHICH IS *THE FOURTH GRADE!* AND WHAT AN *INCREDIBLE* ADVENTURE IT *WILL BE!*

SCRIBBLE SCRIBBLE

45

48

FOR THE *RECORD,* THE *ANSWER* WAS *NO*....

BEFORE I *YAP* ANY MORE, I SHOULD TELL YOU ABOUT SOME OF THE *OTHER* KIDS.

SEE, THE THING IS, WHEN I MET *REGGIE* I THOUGHT, OKAY. HE'S *WEIRD,* BUT I CAN *HANDLE* THAT. I CAN HANG OUT WITH THE *WEIRD KID.* BUT WHAT HAPPENS IF THEY'RE *ALL* THE *WEIRD KIDZ* FOR INSTANCE...

THERE'S *OWEN,* WHO I'M *PRETTY SURE* IS THE CRAZY, *PASTE*-EATING, *BOOGER*-PICKING TYPE...

MARY VIOLET, WHO LOOKS LIKE A FREAKED-OUT *CABBAGE PATCH KID...*

REGGIE'S COUSIN *EARTH DOG* IS *CHUNKY* AND *SLOPPY* AND WRITES POEMS...

AND *BUG* AND *IGGY...* WHO'VE ACTUALLY BEEN PRETTY QUIET SINCE REGGIE *BARFED* ON THEM.

How's it Goin'?

Oh, dear.. Oh, dear...

DON'T *JUDGE* ME.

Leave us ALONE!

SO THERE I AM, SURROUNDED BY *WEIRDOS* AND ALREADY SENT TO THE *PRINCIPAL!*

I DIDN'T THINK THINGS COULD GET *WORSE.*

THEN WE HAD *GYM* CLASS.

49

TWEEEEEEEEEEEEEE

OK, GIRLS, I DON'T KNOW WHAT YOU GET *AWAY* WITH IN YOUR *OTHER* SISSY *CLASSES* . . . BUT IN *HERE* WE WORK *LIKE DOGS! NOW,* VOLUNTEERS!

RHONDA BLEENIE!

EGAD!

AND MARY *VIOLET!*

Oh no.

LISTEN, *AMELIA,* IF I DON'T MAKE IT *BACK,* TELL REGGIE THAT I *LOVED* HIM! WILL YOU *DO* THAT FOR ME? *WILL* YOU?

AMPS 99

HOME

NO.

HOME

THANKS.

WHY AREN'T WE IN THE *GYM?*

THE *GIRLS* HAVE CLASS THERE.

WE'RE SUPPOSED TO MEET DOWN *HERE...*

AN' THEN HEAD OUT TO THE *FIELD.*

SO WHERE'S OL' MAN BIGGERS H...

SHH!

WHAT'S GOING ON?

IS HE *ASLEEP?*

Maybe he's Meditating.

COACH BIGGERS, WE'RE HERE FOR CLASS!

HELLOOOO... COACH BIGGERS? YOO-HOO...

THIS LOOKS *BAD.*

53

55

AND TRY NOT TO *PANIC!*

MS. BARKLEY **KILLED** MARY VIOLET!

MARY VIOLET IS **DEAD!**

GIRLS, WAIT!

NOW, GIRLS, *CALM DOWN.* MARY VIOLET AND I WERE JUST HAVING A LITTLE *FUN!*

T-TELL THEM, *MARY VIOLET!*

Oh, yes, girls, we were only fooling! HA, HA!

THAT WASN'T *MARY VIOLET....* THAT WAS *YOU!*

NO, IT WASN'T.

YES IT WAS! WE SAW YOUR LIPS MOVE!

LOOK, GIRLS, LISTEN TO ME....

PLOP

GASP!

uh-oh.

58

ACTUALLY, THE RECORD IS STILL HELD BY *BOB "STINKY" BLACKHEAD*, CLASS OF '74....

A *LEGEND*.

SO, *ANYWAY*, THE TEACHING STAFF AT MY NEW SCHOOL WAS TURNING OUT TO BE AS *MESSED UP* AS THE *KIDS*. REGGIE HAD TRIED TO *WARN* ME THE NIGHT BEFORE CLASSES WERE SET TO START...

HE TOLD ME ALL ABOUT 'WICKED WITCH' BLOOM...

AND YOUR LITTLE DOG, TOO!

THE TERROR WHTHAT IS 'MAD DOG' BARKLEY...

'TEN SHUN!

NO NECK NORRIS, BUILT LIKE A *GRAPE*, AND MAD AS HECK...

WHADDA YOU LOOKIN' AT?!

AND *OLD MAN* BIGGERS, WHO'S SO OLD HE'S *LEGALLY DEAD* IN SIX STATES

So then noah says "sorry, Zeke, you're gonna have ta 'Dog Paddle'..."

NOW I DON'T LIKE SCHOOL *NORMALLY*. IMAGINE WHAT I THOUGHT ABOUT *THIS* FREAK PARADE. THE ONLY WAY I COULD FALL ASLEEP WAS BY CONVINCING MYSELF THAT REGGIE WAS *EXAGGERATING*.

Amelia's Room!

BUT FOR MAYBE THE *FIRST* TIME IN HIS *LIFE*...

HE WASN'T.

Welcome to **T.R.A.M.P.**
(Teaching Respect and Anger Management in Preteens)

Good afternoon. Welcome to Teaching Respect and Anger Management in Preteens.

I'm Mr. Norris, your teacher.

YOU'RE **RIGHT!** HE REALLY **DOESN'T** HAVE A **NECK!**

I **TOLD** YOU. HE'S **BUILT** LIKE A **HARD-BOILED EGG!**

SNICKER

IS SOMETHING **FUNNY?**

N-No... No, SIR! =GULP= S-Sorry, Sir... G-GO on!

CONTROL... Control... 3... 2... 1...

Fine. On a personal note, I'd like to say that this class holds special *meaning* to me, having spent this summer coming to terms with my own...um... *ISSUES.*

No doubt some of you remember last year's *geography incident?*

Well, I'm **very pleased** to report that doctors were able to remove the world atlas, and little Timmy Fletcher is feeling much better.

Well, anyway, let's just put all of that *behind* us.

Umm... no **pun** intended.

To get started, I thought we'd take a little **"personality test"** to get the feel of the group.

Show of hands... If caught in a disagreement with another, how many of you would...

A. Seek resolution by expressing your opinion verbally yet forcefully.

Hmm...interesting... interesting...

B. Keep silent and attempt to avoid any conflict whatsoever.

Yes, yes... fascinating.

Simply fascinating.

Now how many would...
C. Allow anger and resentment to fester and build, eventually swearing a lifelong vendetta against the other person and all others like them.

Very good, I...

⁉⁉

64

Secretariat Orangejulius (The Common Secret Origin) can occur to anyone at anytime (fig. 1). While going about one's daily business, something out of the ordinary occurs, for example, finding a radioactive ladybug (fig. 2). Usually at this point some unforeseen incident takes place, e.g., the ladybug viciously attacks (fig. 3).

At this point the person undergoing the origin may experience a strange dizziness, combined with a feeling of disorientation and dread (fig. 4). One of two things will occur: the sudden and dramatic appearance of superpowers, propelling the recipient to heights of fame and glory as the latest caped wonder (fig. 5a) or, the sudden and dramatic appearance of death, propelling them to main-course status at the worm buffet (fig. 5b).

Ummm...interesting... but don't you think that's a little unrealistic?

NOT COMPARED TO MY *OTHER* DREAM!

SNICKER!

What, p*harmacy*? All that takes is a little hard work and a few years of higher learning.

SNICKER SNICKER GIGGLE

NO *OFFENSE*, SIR, BUT GIVE ME A FEW *WEEKS*...

SNICKER GIGGLE SNORT SNORT

POUND POUND POUND

AND YOU'LL SEE I HAVE A BETTER CHANCE WITH THE *LADYBUG*.

SNORT

AHAHAHAHAH HAHAHAH HAHAH

HAHAHAHA I KNOW...HA HA...I'M GOING!

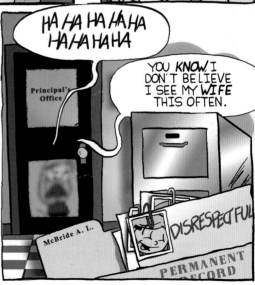

HA HA HA HA HA HA HA HA HA

YOU *KNOW* I DON'T BELIEVE I SEE MY *WIFE* THIS OFTEN.

Principal's Office

McBride A. L.

DISRESPECTFUL

PERMANENT RECORD

SO BASICALLY, THAT WAS THE *DISASTER* AS IT *HAPPENED*....

MY *FIRST DAY* AT MY *NEW* SCHOOL!

THERE WAS ONE *SILVER LINING*, THOUGH....

WE HAVEN'T HAD *GYM* SINCE!

BYE.

JOE McCARTHY ELEMENTARY *"Weeding out the wrong element since 1952"*

BLINK BLINK

BLINK BLINK

CLASS DISMISSED.

Loosely in
Disguise, and
Frightened

SO **SOMEDAY** I HOPE TO HAVE SOME REALLY GREAT, HAPPY, **UP** STORIES TO TELL YOU.

SOMEDAY... JUST NOT **TODAY**.

SEE, THE PLAN WAS TO SPEND HALLOWEEN WITH MY DAD.

I WAS GONNA **VISIT** HIM BACK **HOME**.

HE WAS GONNA THROW A **PARTY** AND INVITE ALL MY OLD **FRIENDS**.

THREE GUESSES HOW **THAT** TURNED OUT.'

THAT WAS THE **PLAN**, ANYWAY.

72

CHECK OUT WHAT *I* CARVED.

IT'S THE *AMAZING SIGNAL!* SO IF YOU'RE IN TROUBLE, JUST LIGHT IT AND IT WILL SEND OUT A *SIGNAL* FOR....

CAPTAIN AMAZING!

RIIIIIGHT...

IF I EVER NEED A LUNATIC, I'LL BE SURE TO CALL.

SO, PAJAMAMAN, WHAT DID YOU CARVE?

AWWW, C'MON! DON'T BE SHY, PM! SHOW US.

! !

NOBODY LIKES A *SHOWOFF.*

BRRPP

73

75

It's *business*, ya know? I know it's not his *fault*.

I'm just sick of getting *pushed around!*

This time I was really *determined* we'd get to spend the *holiday* together.

>SIGH<
But I *guess not*.

And *hey*, it's not like I'm *freaking* out!

Or even that I'm really *mad!* I just want things more *stable!*

The way things *are*, I don't know if I'm *coming* or *going*.

And the minute I figure things *out*, someone's *draggin'* me somewhere *else!*

IT *HURTS!*

YA KNOW, EVEN *TANNER'S* HOUSE JUST FEELS LIKE A PLACE TO *CRASH.*

AND NO MATTER WHAT *HAPPENS,* I FEEL LIKE THE WORST IS YET TO *COME.*

UH-OH.

I'M SORRY I KEEP BABBLING. YOU DON'T NEED THIS.

I SHOULD BE USED TO *DISAPPOINTMENT* ALREADY....*PREPARED!*

I WISH I COULD JUST *BRACE* MYSELF AND TAKE IT WHEN IT *COMES!* BUT I *CAN'T.*

>SIGH< SOMETIMES I FEEL SO *HELPLESS!*

OUCH

WOW, **THANKS**, AMELIA, I... **HEY!** WHAT'S **WRONG?**

YEAH, YOU LOOK **UPSET!**

IT'S JUST MY **STUPID DAD.** HE CANCELLED OUR **STUPID WEEKEND,** CUZ OF THIS **STUPID BUSINESS TRIP** HE HAS TO TAKE TO **STUPID BOSTON.**

OH, WHO **CARES?!** IT WAS **STUPID** ANYWAY!!

GOSH, SHE REALLY SEEMS **UPSET.** I...I ALMOST FEEL **BAD** FOR HER!

OH, SHOOT. MY HAIR'S GETTING ALL **FLOPPY** FROM THE RAIN. I'M GOING **HOME!**

OKAY. I'LL SEE YOU GUYS TOMORROW FOR **TRICK OR TREAT.**

Ouch!

SO, I GUESS I WAS **PRETTY UPSET**, SINCE I WALKED AROUND FOR AN **HOUR**...

WITHOUT **REALIZING** THAT A. IT WAS **POURING** OUT, AND B. I WALKED AWAY FROM **MY OWN HOUSE**. BY THE TIME I GOT HOME, I LOOKED LIKE A NASTY, SOGGY **SEWER RAT**. MOM ALMOST **LOST IT** WHEN SHE SAW ME SLOSHIN' WATER ALL OVER TANNER'S FLOORS.

SHE WAS **PROBABLY** THINKING UP GOOD WAYS TO **KILL ME** TILL **TANNER** STEPPED IN.

SHE **GUESSED** WHAT WAS **BUGGING** ME AND ASKED MOM TO **LAY OFF**.

SO THEY LEFT ME ALONE TO GO **SULK** IN A TUB.

〉HEH HEH〈 THAT'S KIND OF A **PUN**.

SO NOW **MOM** WAS FEELING **SUPERGUILTY** CUZ SHE MADE PLANS WHEN SHE THOUGHT I WAS **GOIN' AWAY**.

AUNT TANNER DIDN'T WANT MY MOM TO CANCEL HER **PLANS**, SO SHE DECIDED TO THROW A **HALLOWEEN PARTY** FOR ME. SHE INVITED A BUNCH OF MY FRIENDS TO COME OVER, AND **ONE** OF THEM EVEN **ANONYMOUSLY** INVITED ME TO GO **TRICK OR TREATING** WITH THEM!

(I KNOW IT WAS **REGGIE**, BUT IT WAS STILL REAL **NICE** OF HIM.)

DING DONG

I'LL GET IT!

OH, IT'S YOU. HOW NICE.

NO DOUBT YOU NOTICE I'M *DRESSED* AS A *BRIDE*.

DO YOU KNOW *WHY?*

BECAUSE *REGGIE* IS GOING AS A *GROOM!* WE'RE GOING AS A *PAIR!* YOU'RE *JEALOUS,* AREN'T YOU? *JEALOUS,* I SAY! *ADMIT IT!*

KNOCK KNOCK

LOOK!

HEY, GUYS! WHAT'S *UP?*

WHAT'S UP? WHAT'S UP? YOU DOOFUS! WHY AREN'T YOU DRESSED LIKE MY GROOM?

RHONDA, DON'T BE SO *HARD* ON HIM. YOU CAN *STILL* GO AS A COUPLE, ONLY *NOW* THE CHARACTER IS MUCH MORE YOUR *STYLE...*

THE BRIDE OF FRANKENSTEIN.

EEP OUT (PLEASE)

KNOCK KNOCK KNOCK

GO AWAY!

HEY, KIDDO. YOU OKAY?

I SAID, GO AWAY!

LISTEN, I KNOW RHONDA REALLY HURT YOUR FEELINGS,

BUT YOU WERE SAYING SOME PRETTY ROUGH THINGS.

I can't believe you're taking HER SIDE!

I'M NOT TAKING HER SIDE.

BUT YOU HAVE TO UNDERSTAN. YOU CAN'T TALK TO YOUR FRIENDS THAT WAY.

SNIFF

OH DEAR. I HOPE THIS ISN'T TOO SCARY.

T'sk— Dames!

I CAN BARELY SEE OVER MY BERRY!

SHH! IT'S ON!

ZOMBIE GORE PART 21

SAY, BABY, YOU DON'T MIND IF WE WALK THROUGH THIS OLD CEMETERY, DO YA?

YOU HAVE SOME NERVE, NOT COMING AS MY GROOM!

I JUST THOUGHT IT WAS A STUPID IDEA! BESIDES, EVERYONE WOULD MAKE FUN OF ME!

WHY IF I DIDN'T KNOW BETTER I'D THINK THAT YOU WERE...

SOMEDAY, YOU'RE GONNA LOSE ME, REGGIE GRABINSKY!

WILL YOU SHUT UP! WE'RE TRYING TO WATCH THE MOVIE!

GROAN

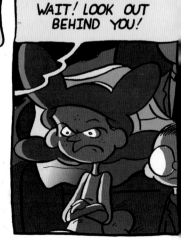

NOW, BABY...WHY WOULD...? WAIT! LOOK OUT BEHIND YOU!

86

SO WHAT D'YA **THINK?**

IT'S **OVER,** ALREADY.

WAS IT GOOD AND **SCARY?**

OH, COME **ON!** YOU'RE **EXAGGERATING!** HOW BAD COULD...!

UMMM... LISTEN, IF YOU KIDS ARE "DAMAGED,

PLEASE, DO THE **RIGHT THING...** BLAME THE **MEDIA.**

ZOMBIE **GORE**

WARNING: This film contains scenes so horrific, violent and gory that it will permanently damage the psyche of any viewer under the age of 18.

"TWO THUMBS UP!"

91

95

WHY ARE WE **STANDING** HERE? THOSE **ZOMBIES** PROBABLY ATE REGGIE'S BRAIN **ALREADY!**

CALM DOWN!

WE JUST GOT SCARED CUZ OF THAT DUMB **MOVIE.** I'M SURE REGGIE'S **OKAY.**

EASY FOR YOU TO SAY! THEY'RE NOT **CHOMPIN'** ON **YOUR** BRAIN!

WILL YOU RELAX! NO **ZOMBIE** ATE REGGIE'S **BRAIN!**

I MEAN, **THINK** ABOUT IT! IT WOULD **BARELY** COUNT AS A **SNACK.**

OKAY...THEN **WHO** WOULD TRY TO **SCARE** US?

LET'S GET 'EM.

SO, THERE YOU GO....EVIL WAS PUNISHED AND GOOD PREVAILED.

HECK, EVEN ME AN' RHONDA GOT ALONG FOR A WHILE!

:SIGH:

SO I DIDN'T GET TO SEE MY DAD, BUT IT'S OKAY. HE FELT REALLY BAD ABOUT IT.

AND MY MOM SAID SHE DIDN'T ENJOY HER PARTY, CUZ SHE FELT TOO GUILTY.

ALL OF THIS MADE ME REALIZE SOMETHING VERY IMPORTANT...

COME CHRISTMASTIME, I CAN BLEED THEM DRY.

SEE YA.

99

Amelia McBride and the Other Side of Yuletide

WELL, HERE WE **ARE.**

THE **SADDEST** NIGHT IN ALL OF **KID-DOM.**

THE NIGHT **AFTER** CHRISTMAS.

AT **NO POINT** IN THE YEAR WILL WE BE **FURTHER** AWAY FROM **NEXT CHRISTMAS** THAN WE ARE **RIGHT NOW.**

USUALLY, I'M **QUEEN** OF THE **AFTER-CHRISTMAS BLUES.**

I DIDN'T GET **ENOUGH**... OR WHAT I **WANTED**... OR... **WHATEVER.**

AND THEN, **WELL**...

THEN I'D GO INTO THIS **MONSTER SULK** THAT'S BEEN KNOWN TO LAST TILL MY **BIRTHDAY!**

FEBRUARY 10, IN CASE YOU'RE **SHOPPING.**

BUT I DON'T **KNOW,** THIS YEAR FEELS **DIFFERENT.**

:SIP:

IT'S HARD TO SAY WHEN THE WHOLE THING **STARTED**...

BUT I GUESS IT BEGAN WITH **REGGIE**...

AND THE DAY HE DECIDED TO FIND OUT THE **TRUTH**...

ABOUT SANTA.

AMELIA, YOU'RE BACK!

YOU WERE AWAY?

FOR THREE DAYS!

SO THAT WAS WHY THE WORLD FELT FULL OF JOY!

HA HA HA

YOU WON'T BE SO SMART WHEN YOU SEE THE PRE-CHRISTMAS LOOT I GOT!

PRE-CHRISTMAS LOOT?

YEAH, FROM MY DAD.

I'VE BEEN WORKIN' ON MY DAD'S DIVORCE GUILT, AND IT PAID OFF.

BIG TIME!

VIDEO GAMES, BARBIES, CDS, CHEMISTRY SET, TELESCOPE.

EASY. BAKE. OVEN.

GASP! THE HOLY GRAIL!

WE HAVE BEEN **TOLD** THAT IF WE ARE **GOOD** THROUGHOUT THE YEAR, COME CHRISTMAS EVE, SANTA WILL **REWARD** US WITH **GIFTS!**

SADLY, THIS IS NOT ALWAYS THE **CASE.**

FOR WITHIN **THIS ORGANIZATION**, A MEMBER (*WHO PREFERS TO REMAIN NAMELESS*)

HAS **NOT** RECEIVED **GIFTS** FOR SOME **THREE YEARS!**

EVEN THOUGH **HE**...

OR **SHE**...

HAS BEEN EXCEEDINGLY GOOD!

WHAT?! NO **TOYS?!** NO **PRESENTS?!** NO... **NOTHING?!**

NONE.

WELL... MAYBE NOT **NONE.**

WITNESS LAST YEAR'S **GIFTS** OF **SOCKS, DEODORANT,** AND **UNDIES.**

GASP

YOU'RE **LYING!** I CAN'T BELIEVE SANTA WOULD STIFF SOMEONE LIKE THAT!

I DON'T BELIEVE IN SANTA AT *ALL!* I THINK HE'S A SHILL FOR *SEARS.*

SHHH!

WHAT IF HE **HEARS** YOU?!

ARE YOU *KIDDING?*

THIS IS OUR **MISSION:** TO DISCOVER WHY **SANTA** IS BEING **UNFAIR.**

FURTHER, WHO IS BEHIND HIS *FUNDING?* DOES HE EVEN *EXIST?* AND *IF SO,* CAN WE *SUE* HIM?

YOU'RE A **DISTURBED** LITTLE BOY, DO YOU **KNOW** THAT?

I **PRIDE** MYSELF ON IT.

SO WHO'S IN? RHONDA? PAJAMAMAN? WHAT ABOUT **YOU,** AMELIA, ARE YOU **WITH** US?

OOOH... I **HATE** PEER PRESSURE!

GREAT.

WATCH OUT, *FAT MAN...*

YOU'RE GOING **DOWN!**

REGGIE COULDN'T HAVE PICKED A **WORSE** YEAR FOR THIS ADVENTURE.

IT LOOKED LIKE I WAS SET TO GRAB A **BIG HAUL.** I COULDN'T AFFORD TO END UP ON THE **NAUGHTY** LIST.

HMM.

OR WORSE YET...

HO HO HO

Obnoxious, Nosy, Doofy

Amelia Louise McBride

OUT OF FEAR OF LOSING ALL MY **SANTA LOOT,** I DECIDED TO **REALLY** WORK MOM.

WH–WHY CAN'T WE BE A FAMILY AGAIN?

D–DON'T YOU GUYS **LOVE** ME?

IN MY FAVOR, I HAD THE IMPRESSIVE BUNCH OF BRIBES–ER, I MEAN, "GIFTS" FROM MY **DAD.**

BELIEVE ME, NO PARENT WANTS TO BE SHOWN UP BY THEIR *EX.*

SO, ARMED WITH A **TOYS 'R' US** CATALOG, I SAW MY **OPPORTUNITY.**

I DECIDED TO SELL IT **HARD.**

109

ALLIANCE FORCES... *CLIK*

NEW DANGER... *CLIK*

VIOLENCE ERUPTED... *CLIK*

ISN'T ANYTHING *DECENT* ON? ANY *CHRISTMAS* PROGRAMMING?

WE'VE GOT *SOFTEE CHICKEN: IT'S A SOFTEE CHRISTMAS* OR THE *NINJA FIGHT SQUADRON'S BUTT-KICKIN' KAWANZA*

AND A NINJA *CLUBHOUSE,*

AND A NINJA *CHOPPER,*

AND A NINJA *BOAT,*

AND A NINJA *CYCLE,*

AND A NINJA *TRUCK,*

!

OOH! NINJA KWANZAA! PLEEEEZ!

NO! I'VE HAD IT UP TO HERE WITH THE *NINJA FIGHT THINGEES,* PEOPLE!

WE'RE WATCHING *SOFTEE CHICKEN!* RIGHT, TANNER?

TANNER?

I DUNNO.... I MEAN, *NINJA KWANZAA!*

FORGET IT! *CLIK*

OH, NO, MR ELF. DID SANTA REALLY GET *CONTAMINATED MAIL?*

YEP! IT LOOKS LIKE WE'LL HAVE TO CANCEL CHRISTMAS!

NOT IF MY FRIEND LUCKY SQUIRREL AND I HAVE ANYTHING TO SAY ABOUT IT! LET'S GO!

IF YOU DON'T *MIND,* I'LL JUST DO A LITTLE *READING.*

AHEM!

AND A NINJA *CARPORT,*

AND A NINJA *CANTINA,*

AMELIA, I **KNOW** WHAT YOU'RE **DOING**.

WHAT? WHAT ARE YOU **TALKING** ABOUT?!

YOU CAN'T **PLAY** ME, YOUNG LADY!

WOW!! I THINK IT'S TIME TO CHECK ON THE **IMAGINARY CAKE** I'M PRETENDING TO BAKE.

MOM... I...

LOOK, **SWEETIE**, I'M **GLAD** YOUR DAD BOUGHT YOU ALL THOSE **GIFTS!** REALLY, I **AM**.

BUT I CAN'T **DO** THAT.

WE JUST **DON'T HAVE THE MONEY!** WE NEED TO SAVE FOR A **HOUSE!** WE CAN'T IMPOSE ON TANNER **FOREVER**.

LISTEN, I **KNOW** YOU'VE BEEN **GOOD**, AND IN SPITE OF **EVERYTHING**, YOU'VE HELD IT **TOGETHER**. BUT YOU'LL HAVE TO BE **CONTENT** WITH WHATEVER **SANTA** BRINGS.

THIS WAS A **DISTURBING CONVERSATION**.

FIRST I DISCOVER THAT I'M **POOR!** NOT ONLY THAT, I'M A **TANNER TANTRUM** AWAY FROM BEING **HOMELESS!**

SECOND, MOM IS BUYING ME **NO GIFTS AT ALL!** I HAVE TO RELY ON **SANTA**.

WHICH WOULD BE **FINE**, IF HE DOES, IN FACT, **EXIST**, AND IF I SOMEHOW **ESCAPED** BEING NAMED **NAUGHTY**.

WHICH, AS YOU'RE ABOUT TO SEE, WAS NOT **LIKELY**.

GREETINGS, G.A.S.P. MEMBERS.

WELCOME TO THE WAR ROOM.

I HAD **NO IDEA** THIS CLUB HOUSE WAS A **SPLIT LEVEL.**

PM AND I WORKED **ALL DAY** PREPARING THESE **PLANS.**

WE THINK THEY SPELL OUT **OPERATION ELFWATCH** PRETTY CLEARLY.

DOES ANYONE HAVE ANY **QUESTIONS?**

YEAH, DID THIS **REALLY** TAKE YOU **ALL DAY?**

HA HA HA

ARE THERE ANY **OTHER** QUESTIONS?

THAT AREN'T SARCASTIC!

115

LATER THAT AFTERNOON WE STOPPED BY **PAJAMAMAN'S HOUSE**. I HAD NEVER BEEN THERE BEFORE, AND IT WASN'T WHAT I **EXPECTED**.

THE PLACE WAS **TINY** AND KIND OF A **MESS**. IT WAS PRETTY **OBVIOUS** HIS FOLKS DIDN'T HAVE MUCH **MONEY**. I HAD BEEN FEELING SORTA SORRY FOR MYSELF AFTER WHAT MY MOM SAID, BUT SUDDENLY I WAS FEELING PRETTY **LUCKY**.

WHILE PM WAS OUT OF THE ROOM, I NOTICED THIS **CLIPPING** FROM A CATALOG TAPED TO THE FRIDGE. IT CAUGHT MY EYE CUZ IT WAS FOR THE **RED CAPTAIN NINJA** THAT WAS AT THE TOP OF **MY** WANT LIST. I REALLY THOUGHT DAD WOULD **COME THROUGH** WITH IT, BUT I GUESS THEY'RE PRETTY HARD TO FIND.

I HAD **NO** IDEA PM WAS...

POOR AS DIRT?

HE'S A LATCHKY KID, YOU KNOW.

WHAT'S THAT?

YOU'VE NEVER HEARD OF A LATCHKY KID?

Latchicus Keykidius (the Common Latchky Kid) The Latchkys were a group of children descended from Polish nobility who lived in Warsaw durring the time of the Cold War. To protect themselves from the freezing temperatures brought on by this war, they wore big hats (fig. 1). Disgusted by their treatment at the hands of Communism and appalled by the state of modern polka music, the Latchkys fled Warsaw in the middle of the night (fig. 2). Not being able to afford passage on a ship, the Latchkys were forced to swim the icy Atlantic, buffered from the elements only by their brains, their raw courage, and their big hats (fig. 3).

(fig1)

(fig2)

(fig3)

Upon finally reaching the shores of America, the Latchkys quickly forgot their past hardships, and, throwing off their waterlogged clothing, danced butt nekkid (except of course for the hats) in the streets (fig. 4). Their descendents (including Pajamaman) live in the US to this day, where they remain free to express their love of liberty, polka, and big hats.

(Fig. 4)

YOU DO KNOW WHAT A **LATCH KEY** KID **REALLY** IS, RIGHT?

YEAH, IT'S JUST MORE **FUN** THIS WAY.

THINGS WENT ON AS USUAL, AND CHRISTMAS KEPT GETTING *CLOSER*.

BUT NO MATTER *WHAT*, I COULDN'T STOP THINKING ABOUT *PAJAMAMAN'S HOUSE* AND THAT STUPID CLIPPING.

I ASKED *REGGIE* ABOUT IT, AND HE SAID PM WAS PROBABLY *HINTING* THAT HE WANTED IT FOR *CHRISTMAS*...

BUT THERE WAS NO CHANCE HE WOULD GET IT.

ATTENTION ALL **NINJA** FIGHT SQUADRON

ACTION FIGURES

RED CAPTAIN NINJA®

$14.9

IT WAS WEIRD.

I WAS JUST USED TO THESE GUYS BEING MY FRIENDS. I NEVER THOUGHT ABOUT WHO WAS RICH OR POOR.

AND EVEN THOUGH I FELT *BAD* FOR PM, I STILL *REALLY WANTED* A MOUNTAIN OF PRESENTS FOR *ME*. WHICH PROBABLY PUT ME AT THE TOP OF A *NEW LIST*....

Whiny Self-Centered Jerks

AMELIA LOUISE McBRIDE

CELINE DION

P. DIDDY

ADD TO THIS THE NAGGING QUESTION OF WHY SANTA WOULD IGNORE SOMEONE LIKE PAJAMAMAN, AND THERE WAS ONLY ONE THING I COULD DO....

WHEN I WAS A *KID,* I REALLY LIKED THIS SONG, *"STILL ROCK 'N' ROLL TO ME."*

IT'S BY *BILLY JOEL,* AND ONE OF THE REASONS I *LIKED* IT, THE *BIG REASON,* REALLY, WAS *ONE LINE:*

"YOU SHOULDN'T TRY TO BE A STRAIGHT-A STUDENT IF YOU ALREADY THINK TOO MUCH."

HEH, HEH THAT'S *PRETTY GOOD.*

I THOUGHT SO! IT WAS, LIKE, MY *MOTTO* FOR YEARS!

BUT THE THING *IS,* ONE DAY I READ THE *LYRICS* AND THEY WERE *COMPLETELY DIFFERENT!*

"SHOULD I TRY TO BE A STRAIGHT-A STUDENT? IF YOU ARE, **THEN** YOU THINK TOO MUCH."

I WAS *DEVASTATED!*

I-I CAN'T GO ON.

WHATSAMATUH WIT DA CLOTHES AHM WEARIN'?

NO LOITER

GLASS HOUSES

BILLY JOEL

BUT EVEN *KNOWING* THE NEW *LYRICS,* IT NEVER REPLACED THE ONE I'D *MADE UP!*

DO YOU KNOW WHAT I'M *SAYING?*

UM... YEAH. SANTA IS LIKE BILLY JOEL... AND THE LYRICS ARE RUDOLPH, AND...

ACTUALLY, *NO.*

ALL I CAN *TELL* YOU IS WHAT *I* THINK.

AND THE *TRUTH IS,* I BELIEVE IN SANTA *NOW,* PROBABLY *MORE* THAN WHEN I WAS *LITTLE.*

THERE IS REAL *MAGIC* AT CHRISTMAS, YA *KNOW?* I MEAN, IT'S COMPLETELY *CORNY,* AND I'D PROBABLY BE STRIPPED OF MY REPLACEMENTS *FAN CLUB MEMBERSHIP* FOR SAYING SO, BUT IT'S *TRUE.* AND ANY TIME YOU *FIND* MAGIC IN THIS WORLD, YOU HAVE TO *FIGHT HARD* TO KEEP IT.

I THINK WHAT YOU'RE *REALLY* ASKING, THOUGH, IS WHY ISN'T LIFE *FAIR.* AND I'M *SORRY,* SWEETIE, BUT I DON'T HAVE AN *ANSWER.* BUT LISTEN, YOU SHOULDN'T HAVE SUCH A *HEAVY HEART* ON CHRISTMAS EVE. SO *CLOSE YOUR EYES,* AND BE *CERTAIN* THAT SANTA IS ON HIS WAY.

AND WHEN YOU *SLEEP,* DREAM OF ALL THE *GIFTS* YOU *WILL* RECEIVE.

AND THE ONES YOU *ALREADY HAVE.*

I RULE!

I KNEW THE FAT GUY WOULDN'T LET ME DOWN! NOW LET'S SEE... HOW ABOUT WE START WITH...

THIS ONE!

RIP
TEAR
SHRED
TEAR
RIP

A *HAT*? LET'S HOPE THIS IS A LITTLE *ELFIN* HUMOR.

AH, THIS LITTLE *BEAUTY* IS A *KEEPER.* I CAN FEEL IT!

RIP
TEAR
SHRED
TEAR
RIP

I CAN'T *BELIEVE* YOU GOT *RED* CAPTAIN NINJA!

HEY, GUYS. WHAT'S UP?

AMELIA, COME ON IN! YOU WON'T BELIEVE WHAT HAPPENED!

THERE IS A SANTA! PM PROVED IT!

HE *SAW* HIM LEAVING HIS *HOUSE!*

HE SAID HE WAS KINDA *SHORT,* BUT IT WAS *DEFINITELY HIM!*

HE EVEN *DROPPED* HIS *HAT!*

"THERE IS A SANTA."

HEARING THAT MADE ME *HAPPIER* THAN I'D BEEN IN A *LONG* TIME.

CUZ *LAST* CHRISTMAS, I LIVED WITH MY MOM *AND* DAD ON WEST 86TH STREET IN *MANHATTAN*.

NOW, I LIVE WITH MY MOM AND *HER SISTER* IN, LIKE, *NOWHERE*, PENNSYLVANIA.

AND THAT'S *FINE*. REALLY IT *IS*.

IT'S JUST THAT SOMETIMES I *MISS* THE WAY THINGS *USED* TO BE.

AND I *WISH* THAT I COULD GO *BACK*.

BUT, *REALLY*, I KNOW THAT EVEN IF I *COULD*...

IT WOULDN'T BE THE SAME.

BUT *ENOUGH* OF THAT. *THIS* TIME WE'RE HAVING A *HAPPY* ENDING!

Speak Softee
to Me

THE FUNNY THING IS, IT *USED* TO BE SPRING!

LIKE, TWO *DAYS* AGO, IT WAS *BEAUTIFUL* AND TODAY, *POW!* WINTER WONDERLAND.

NOT THAT I *MIND.* A GOOD SNOW DAY BEATS A *MATH QUIZ* HANDS DOWN.

AMELIA, COME INSIDE!

>TSK< SITTING ON THE STEPS IN THE *SNOW!* YOU'LL CATCH YOUR *DEATH* OF *COLD.*

I GUESS A COLD FANNY IS THE LEADING CAUSE OF DEATH AMONG NINE-YEAR-OLDS.

138

Hi, this is Tanner Clark, and since you have this unlisted number, I probably would like to talk to you....

Unfortunately, I'm not home right now, so please leave your...

WHAT'S THE *LICENSING DEPARTMENT?*

WELL, WE DECIDE *WHO* GETS TO MAKE SOFTEE CHICKEN *MERCHANDISE.*

YOU KNOW, LIKE, IF SOMEONE WANTS TO MAKE A *TOY,* *WE* HAVE TO *APPROVE* IT.

GOSH! IT MUST BE HARD DECIDING WHAT STUFF TO MAKE.

WELL, IT *USED* TO BE....WE WERE VERY *PICKY.*

NOW, WE PRETTY MUCH RUBBER-STAMP ANY *LAME IDEA* THAT COMES ALONG.

EXCEPT THIS *ONE* IDEA FOR SOFTEE CHICKEN *FROZEN CHICKEN DINNERS!*

I THOUGHT IT WAS *DISGUSTING,* BUT MY *BOSS* LOVED IT.

BOY! WE HAD A BIG FIGHT ABOUT *THAT* ONE!

>HEH HEH< WE MUST'VE GONE BACK AND FORTH FOR **MONTHS**.

REMEMBER **THAT**, AMELIA? **AMELIA**?

OH, **IGNORE** HER, MR. McBRIDE. SHE'S ALWAYS **GROUCHY** IN THE **MORNING**.

YEAH, I...I GUESS **THAT'S** IT.

WHAT'S **THIS** TOY?

HMMM? OH...THAT'S THE **SOFTEE TALKIE**.

WE THOUGHT **WALKIE-TALKIES** WOULD BE A BIG **HIT** WITH KIDS.

TILL WE REALIZED MOST OF 'EM HAVE **CELL PHONES**.

WALKIE-TALKIES, EH? THEY COULD COME IN HANDY WITH MY **CRIME FIGHTING**.

MY **LAST** SET WAS CONFISCATED BY **SANTA CLAUS** WHEN I TRIED TO **BUST** HIM.

WE STOPPED THE CAR AND *EVENTUALLY* WE FOUND THE COMIC, ONLY NOW IT WAS MORE A *40¢ COMIC*. *AND* PAJAMAMAN SPENT THE *REST* OF THE TRIP PUNCHING HIMSELF IN THE *FOREHEAD*.

YA KNOW, THIS IS TURNING OUT TO BE A PRETTY *LAME* SNOW DAY. EVERYONE ELSE IS *SICK,* CUZ ON THE LAST DAY OF OUR TRIP, RHONDA FELL OUT OF THE *BOAT,* GOT SOAKING *WET,* CAUGHT A *COLD,* AND THEN *GAVE* IT TO EVERYONE ELSE.

LUCKILY, I'VE BEEN, IM...IM... IMMU...

A-CHOO!

SORRY, BUT: "*EVERYTHING* COUNTS WHEN YOU'RE BUILDING A HOUSE."

"EVEN IF IT *IS* TIGER'S FAULT."

SIGH

A LOT OF TIMES, I HAVE *NO IDEA* WHAT SHE'S *TALKING* ABOUT.

SO WHAT DO YOU WANT *ME* TO DO?

♪ SING YOU A *LULLABY?* ♪

I STILL HAVE ANOTHER *SHOE.*

FINE... WHAT DO YOU WANT TO DO?

I DON'T KNOW, IS THERE SOMETHING *YOU* WANT TO DO?

YES.

SLEEP.

GOOD... CARDS IT IS.

YA KNOW, YOU'RE A—

STOMP STOMP STOMP

WHAT'S THAT?

RUSTLE RUSTLE RUSTLE

IT'S COMING IN!

WAP! WAP! WAP! WAP! WAP! WAP! WAP! WAP!

SMAK! SMAK! SMAK! SMAK! SMAK! SMAK! SMAK! SMAK! SMAK!

OOPS.

Hi, Girls...

Was Hapnennnn...?

REGGIE, THIS IS THE *GIRLS'* TENT!

LET'S KEEP *HITTIN'* HIM.

GEEZ...WILL YOU TWO *RELAX*? I JUST COULDN'T *SLEEP*.

PAJAMAMAN WAS SNORING, AND YOUR DAD'S FEET SMELL LIKE *STALE CHEESE* AND *MOTOR OIL*.

CONGRATULATIONS, AMELIA! HE *IS* YOUR *REAL FATHER*!

HOW'D YOU LIKE TO *SLEEP* IN THE LAKE, SMART MOUTH?!

LADIES, PLEASE!

CAN WE *PLEASE* DO SOMETHING *CIVIL*?

C'MON, GUYS, PLEASE!

PLEASE!

FINE.

SEE, I KNEW YOU WOULDN'T LEAVE ME!

WHY WOULD ANYONE WANT TO BE APART FROM ALL THIS CHARM?

AM I RIGHT?

LOOK, GUYS, I'M SORRY, IT'S JUST THIS TRIP, IT'S... NOT WHAT I EXPECTED.

I DIDN'T MEAN TO BE SUCH A JERK.

AND, LIKE, ON A SCALE OF *ONE* TO *AMELIA*, WITH ONE BEING GOOD AND AMELIA BEING THE *WORST*...

SHE'S AMELIA PLUS *FIVE!*

BUT MY PARENTS *DON'T GET IT!*

I MEAN, SHE CAN BE DOING THE MOST *DISGUSTING* THINGS...

AND ALL THEY SEE IS *ST. REENIE* THE *ARCHANGEL!*

THE *WORST*, THOUGH, IS THAT LAST YEAR THEY GOT IT IN THEIR HEADS TO ENTER HER IN THESE *JUNIOR BEAUTY PAGEANTS.* WELL, ONCE SHE GOT HER FIRST RIBBON, THAT WAS *IT!* NOW ALL MY FOLKS DO IS HAUL HER AROUND TO THESE STUPID *COMPETITIONS* SO SHE CAN GET MORE *TROPHIES.* AND THE *REALLY* AGGRAVATING THING IS SHE KEEPS *WINNING* BECAUSE (AND I'LL GIVE HER THIS) SHE *SINGS* LIKE AN *ANGEL.*

SO ONE NIGHT I GOT SENT TO MY ROOM FOR ASKING IF REENIE EVER WON *BEST IN SHOW.* I WAS SO *MAD* I COULDN'T SLEEP, SO I JUST LAY THERE STEWING. THEN, WHEN EVERYONE WAS ASLEEP, I *SNUCK* INTO REENIE'S ROOM AND DID *THE WORST THING. I'VE EVER DONE...* I SABOTAGED HER *LIP GLOSS!*

IT WASN'T EVEN LIKE IT WAS ME!

THE NEXT DAY, I DIDN'T EVEN REMEMBER DOING IT, BUT THAT NIGHT WE WERE AT ONE OF REENIE'S COMPETITIONS.

PAWT PAWT PAWT PAWT

TAPTY TAP TAP TAP TAP TAPTY TAP

WHILE ONE OF THE OTHER GIRLS WAS HOOFING HER WAY THROUGH THIS TRAIN WRECK OF A TAP DANCE ROUTINE, REENIE WENT IN FOR HER PRE-PERFORMANCE GLOSS UP.

I TOTALLY FREAKED! I WANTED TO STOP HER, BUT IT WAS TOO LATE! REENIE KNEW SOMETHING WAS WRONG... BUT SHE COULDN'T SAY ANYTHING (OBVIOUSLY). I WENT TO MY SEAT AND WAITED FOR REENIE TO GO ON.

REENIE CAME OUT ON STAGE, AND EVERYTHING LOOKED *NORMAL*.

THEN THE MUSIC STARTED, BUT THERE WAS *NO SINGING* COMING FROM REENIE. SHE LOOKED *TERRIFIED!*

BUT SHE KNEW THE SHOW MUST GO ON, SO SHE STARTED TRYING TO FORCE *SOME KIND OF* SOUND OUT OF HER MOUTH.

IT WAS *NO USE!* HER LIPS WERE GLUED SHUT! BUT SHE KEPT *PUSHING* AND *PUFFING* AND *BLOWING!*

TILL IT LOOKED LIKE SHE WAS GONNA *POP.*

THEN FINALLY...

SHE DID.

YIKES!

SO DO YOU *SEE* WHY YOU SHOULD *FEEL* BETTER?

NO.

WELL, YOU WERE WORRIED ABOUT BEING A *JERK*, BUT *REENIE* IS *JUST AS MUCH* OF A JERK, AND I CAN BE AN EVEN *BIGGER* JERK IF I *WANT TO!* SO YOU SHOULDN'T FEEL *BAD*, BECAUSE WE'RE ALL *JUST A BUNCH OF JERKS!* IN FACT, MAYBE EVERYONE IN THE WHOLE *WORLD* IS A JERK!

ISN'T THAT *GREAT?!*

WHAT?

WHAT?!

WHAT?

159

RHONDA'S STORY DIDN'T REALLY MAKE ME *FEEL BETTER*, IT PRETTY MUCH JUST *CREEPED ME OUT*.

SO I JUST SAT UP *ALL NIGHT* GETTING MORE AND MORE *MISERABLE*.

HOOSH

I DON'T KNOW *WHY* I WAS *ACTING* THAT WAY. MAYBE I WAS *POSSESSED!* OR MAYBE I'M JUST A *JERK*.

I MEAN, I LOVE MY *DAD* AND ALL, IT'S *JUST... HMM...* IT'S HARD WRITING *BACKWARD!*

IT'S JUST THAT HE LIVES SO FAR *AWAY* NOW. I FEEL LIKE I NEVER GET TO *SEE* HIM.

SO WHEN I *DO* SEE HIM, I WANT IT TO JUST BE THE *TWO* OF US.

AAH. I *KNOW!* I *KNOW!* I'M A *SELFISH BRAT!* IT'S NOT MY *DAD'S* FAULT.

MAYBE IT'S BECAUSE I'M AN *ONLY* CHILD.

WHICH I GUESS *TECHNICALLY* PUTS THE BLAME BACK ON HIM AND *MOM*.

HMMM... YA KNOW, I *KINDA* FEEL BETTER *ALREADY*.

YOU WILL DO AS *I SAY*.

BECAUSE I KNOW THINGS AREN'T *PERFECT*, AND I KNOW *I'M* NOT PERFECT...

BUT I *ALSO* KNOW THAT I'M STILL YOUR *FATHER*. *UNDERSTAND?*

I *SAID*, DO YOU *UNDERSTAND?*

YES, SIR.

AMELIA, I DON'T KNOW *WHAT* TO *DO*.

I BROUGHT YOUR *FRIENDS* BECAUSE I WANTED TO *MEET* THEM.

PLUS I THOUGHT *YOU'D* LIKE IT.

?

BUT THE WAY YOU *ACT*...

WHY DID YOU WANT TO MEET *THEM?*

BECAUSE THEY'RE A PART OF YOUR *LIFE*.

AND I MAY BE YOUR *DAD*...

BUT I *HAVEN'T* FELT LIKE A VERY BIG PART OF YOUR *LIFE*.

AT LEAST NOT *LATELY*.

LOOK, DAD, I'M *SORRY.* I REALLY *AM.*

I GUESS... I GUESS I WAS SCARED.

CUZ I–I GUESS I SOMETIMES *WORRY.*

THAT MAYBE THE WHOLE *DIVORCE* THING...

WAS CUZ YOU DIDN'T WANT TO BE WITH *ME.*

AMELIA! YOU *KNOW* THAT'S NOT TRUE.

YEAH...WELL... I DON'T KNOW. IT SEEMED THAT WAY *SOMETIMES.*

I... I DON'T KNOW WHAT TO *SAY,* AMELIA.

EXCEPT THAT IT'S NOT *TRUE.*

YOUR *MOM* AND I AREN'T TOGETHER FOR A *LOT* OF REASONS, BUT *NONE* OF THEM ARE YOU.

LOOK... I KNOW THINGS HAVEN'T BEEN THAT *GREAT,* BUT WE CAN *WORK* ON *THAT.* WHAT DO YOU *SAY?*

>SIGH< YEAH. OKAY.

LIFE IS LIKE A *NEW YORK EGG CREAM!*

IT HAS THE *CHOCOLATY GOODNESS* OF *U-BET* SYRUP...

THE *WHOLESOME FORTIFICATION* OF 2% MILK...

THE...UH...THE BUBBLES OF...UM... *SELTZER WATER...*

AND... UH...

OKAY, I WAS *STRETCHING.* LIFE IS *NOTHING* LIKE AN EGG *CREAM.*

IT *SHOULD* BE, THOUGH! AN *EGG CREAM* WOULDN'T MAKE ME SPEND THE NIGHT IN A *TENT* WITH *RHONDA!*

BUT IF LIFE *WERE* AN EGG *CREAM,* MAYBE IT WOULDN'T *CONTAIN* EGG CREAMS, AND WE'D ALL HAVE TO DRINK *YOO-HOO!*

I *KNOW.* SOMETIMES I CAN BE PRETTY *DEEP*.... BUT YOU'LL JUST *HAVE* TO TRY AND KEEP *UP!*

Jimmy Gownley's **AMELIA RULES!**™

Join Amelia and the gang for adventures, mishaps, and homework.

Collect them all!